S0-AWR-389

1 2 3 4 5 6 7 8

First published in the United States 1999
by Dial Books for Young Readers
A division of Penguin Putnam Inc.
345 Hudson Street
New York, New York 10014

Published in Belgium 1997 as *Le Papa Qui Avait 10 Enfants*
Copyright © 1997 by Casterman
All rights reserved
Printed in Mexico.
First Edition
1 3 5 7 9 10 8 6 4 2

Library of Congress Cataloging in Publication Data
Guettier, Bénédicte.
The father who had 10 children/story and pictures
by Bénédicte Guettier.—1st ed.
p.   cm.
Summary: After working hard to take care of his ten children,
a devoted father plans to get away by himself—until he decides
that something is missing.
ISBN 0-8037-2446-2 (trade)
[1 Father and child—Fiction.] I. Title.
PZ7.G93824Fat   1999   [E]—dc21   98-36170
CIP   AC

THE FATHER WHO HAD 9 10 CHILDREN

story and pictures
by
Bénédicte Guettier

Dial Books for Young Readers
New York

ONCE UPON a time
THERE WaS a FATHER
WHO HaD 10 CHiLDReN.

EVERY MORNING HE WOKE UP VERY EARLY AND COOKED 10 BREAKFASTS.

He HELPeD His 10 CHiLDReN PUt on
10 LittLe PaiRs of UNDeRPANts,
10 LittLe T-SHiRts,

10 little pairs of jeans,
20 little socks, and
20 little shoes.

When his 10 children were dressed, he put them all in the car...

AND DROVE THEM TO SCHOOL.

THEN HE DROVE HIMSELF to WORK.

AFTER WORK HE PICKED UP HIS 10 CHILDREN, TOOK THEM HOME, AND GAVE THEM A BATH.

FOR tHEIR DINNER HE MADE
10 FRIED EGGS,
10 BOWLS OF SPAGHETTI,
20 MEATBALLS,
50 BROCCOLI SPEARS, AND
100 RASPBERRIES ...
WITH WHIPPED CREAM.

AFTER DINNER He FLUFFED UP
10 PILLOWS, TOLD
1 BEDtiME STORY, AND GAVE
10 GOOD-NiGHt kisses.

BY NOW THE FATHER WAS VERY TIRED, BUT....

He STAYED UP LATE EVERY NIGHT, WORKING ALL BY HIMSELF ON a SECRET PROJECT.

WHeN it was FiNiSHED, He
SHOWED it to HiS 10 CHilDReN.
THeY HaD NeVeR SeeN SUCH
a BeauTiFul Boat.

THE FATHER LEFT HIS
10 CHILDREN WITH THEIR
GRANDMOTHER. THEN HE SET
OFF ALL BY HIMSELF TO SAIL
AROUND THE WORLD FOR
10 DAYS, OR MAYBE EVEN
10 MONTHS!

ON THE FIRST DAY
HE RESTED...

AND FISHED.

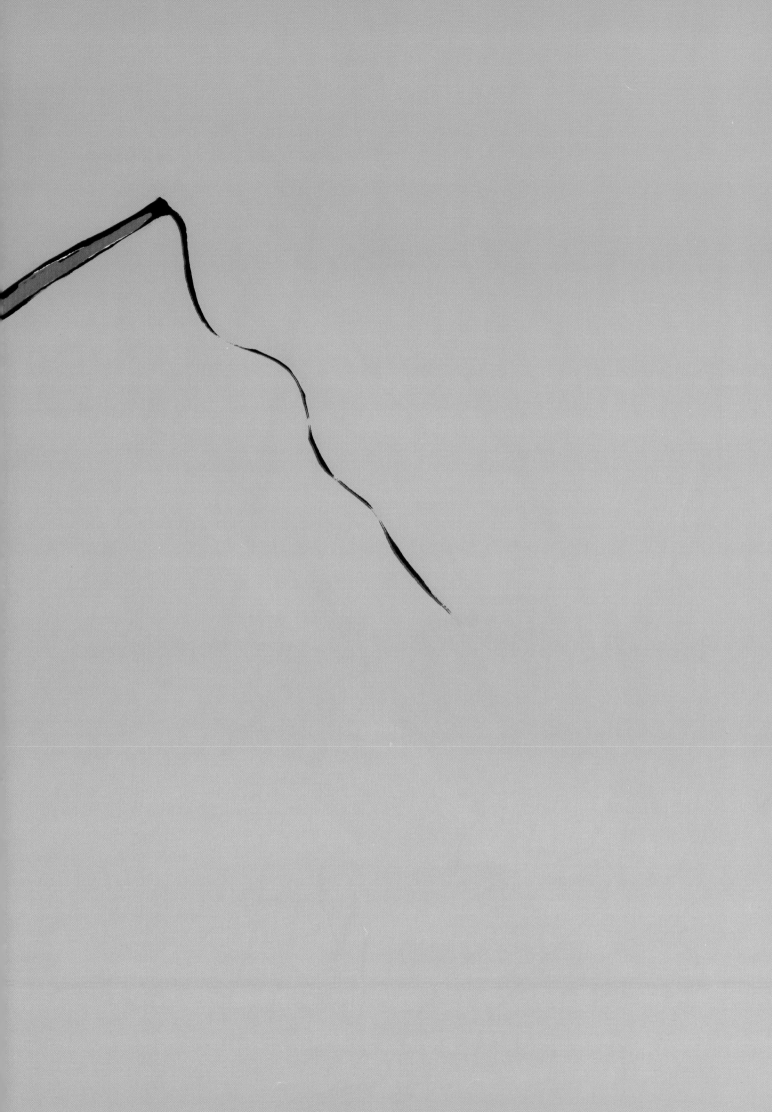

WHEN it GOT DARK,
HE WENT to BED.

THe NeXt MORNING He
WOKe UP VERY EARLY...

AND BEGAN to MAKE BREAKfast.

10 little cups...
10 little...
But something
was missing!

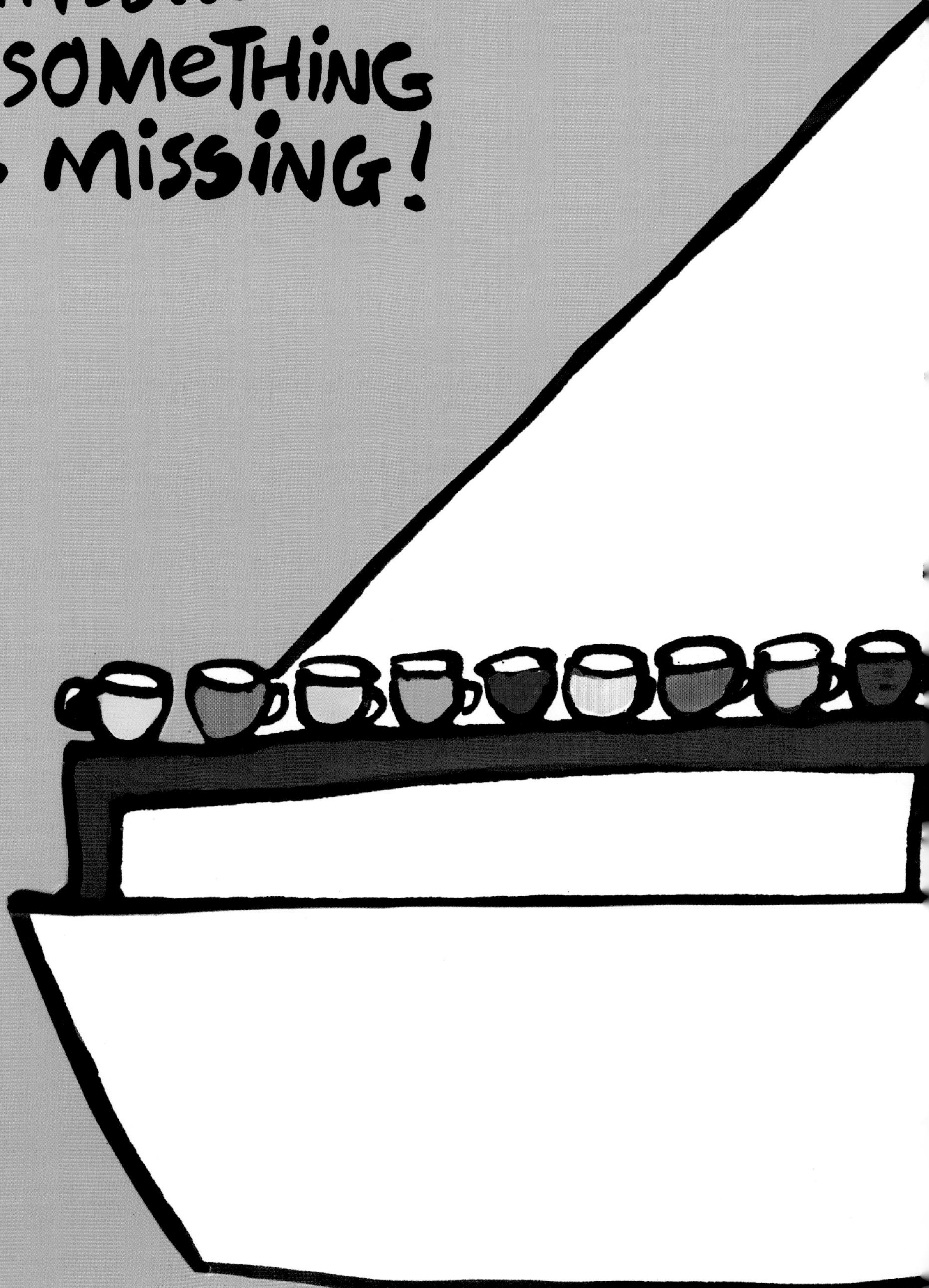

He sailed right back to the shore. "Ahoy, mateys," he called. "Breakfast is ready!"

The 10 children climbed
aboard with their father,

and **TOGETHER** they set off to sail AROUND the WORLD.